·Favorite Fairy Tales·

Golden Goose

Retold by Rochelle Larkin   **Illustrated by Yvette Banek**

The Playmore/Waldman® is a registered trademark of Playmore Inc. Publishers
and Waldman Publishing Corp., New York, New York

The Playmore/Waldman Bug Logo® is a registered trademark of Playmore Inc. Publishers
and Waldman Publishing Corp., New York, New York

Once upon a time there were three brothers. The two older ones were often mean to the youngest, whom they called Simpleton.

But Simpleton was always nice, even to people he didn't know. Once he met an elf in the forest, and Simpleton shared his food with the little man.

As a reward, the elf told Simpleton to dig beneath a certain tree. When he did, he found a goose, perfectly made of solid gold, head and feet and feathers and all.

Tucking the golden goose under his arm, Simpleton
went off to see the world. When it got dark, he stopped at a
roadside inn. The innkeeper and his three daughters were
amazed to see Simpleton's golden goose.

"I must have a feather from that goose," the eldest said to her sisters. She grabbed at a feather, but found she was stuck fast and couldn't let go.

"Sisters, sisters, help me!" she called. But as soon as one and then the other tried to pull her away, they became stuck fast, too.

When Simpleton came back, he paid his bill and
collected his goose. But as he strolled down the road, the
three sisters were pulled right along with him.

A pastor, happening by, saw them and thought the sisters were
running after Simpleton.

"Stop, stop, young ladies!" he cried out. "That's no way to behave!" But as he tried to get hold of the third sister, he became stuck fast too.

Just then, the sexton came out of his house.

"Where are you going, pastor?" he called.

"Help me, help me!" shouted the pastor, but as the sexton tried to pull him loose, he became stuck too.

So they all went along, until at last they came
to the town where the king's palace was.

Now this king had a problem. His only child was the princess, who should have been the happiest girl in the world. But she wasn't.

The king gave her everything in the world.
But the princess never laughed.

A strange curse had been put on her when she was born, that she would never laugh until she met the man she was to marry.

So when she grew up, the king issued a proclamation, offering her hand in marriage and half of his kingdom to boot, to the man who could make the princess laugh.

They came from far and wide. Princes and plain people, young and old, rich and poor. All manner of men came to try and make the princess laugh.
But no one could.

It didn't matter if they were as silly as monkeys or as funny as clowns. No one could make the   princess laugh.

As Simpleton and all the people attached to his goose came into town, the people stared in amazement. No one had ever seen such a sight before.

"Show the princess!" someone shouted at Simpleton.

As they made their way through the town, large crowds gathered along the roadsides, all the way to the king's palace.

They cheered and they jeered until the whole town was filled with shouts and shrieks and screams of laughter.

There was so much noise that the sound carried into the palace itself. The princess came to the window to see what was happening.

She saw the boy and the goose and the others twisting and turning every which way to get loose. But the more they tried, the faster went Simpleton, so that the others were tumbling and tripping all over themselves as they went along.

The roar of the crowds grew greater than ever, but soon there came a new sound.

It rang through the palace, echoing off the walls. It rose above the roar of the crowds, louder than bells pealing, louder than thunder booming.

The king, hearing it, went to find where it was coming from. He found the princess at her window, doubled over with laughter, pointing at Simpleton.

The king didn't laugh, but his smile was as wide as a house. "Bring me that young man here," he ordered.

The king joined their hands together.

"My daughter and half the kingdom," he said, and Simpleton and the princess lived happily, *very* happily, ever after.